CW00828557

BE KIND

How One Kind Act
Can Change the World

Written by
Joann Cebulski

Illustrated by
Colleen Finn

Copyright © 2021 by Joann Cebulski
All rights reserved. No part of this book may be reproduced, scanned,
or distributed in any printed or electronic form without permission.
First Edition: December 2021
Printed in the United States of America
ISBN: 979-8-9853628-0-0
LCCN: 2021924204

To Mom –
Whose kindness changed the world every day

There was a little bee named Busy.

Busy was small...

...and the world seemed
very, very BIG...
and a little lonely.

Busy set out across the meadow
to see what he could see.

Soon Busy came upon
a beautiful butterfly.

"Hi, Miss Butterfly. I'm Busy.
How are you?"

"My wing is bent
and I cannot fly,"
said the butterfly.
"I don't know
what I will do."

"I'll help," said Busy.
He flapped his wings very fast
and got the wrinkles out
of Miss Butterfly's wing.

"Oh, thank you, Busy.
My beautiful wing is good as new!
Now I can visit the flowers
and fly to see my family."

"You are welcome, Miss Butterfly," said Busy.
"I hope to see you again."

Busy continued on his way,
feeling a little less lonely than before.

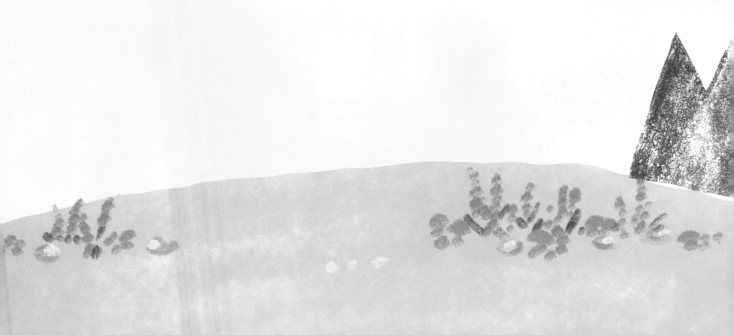

Soon he came upon a caterpillar
looking confused.

"Hi, I'm Busy. Why the big frown,
Mr. Caterpillar?"

"I have many shoes to tie,
but no hands and only feet,"
said the caterpillar.
"I'm not sure what to do."

"No problem," said Busy. "I can help."
Busy helped tie the caterpillar's shoes
and they both looked on with satisfied smiles.

"Thank you, Busy. Your kind act makes me
feel ready to climb the highest tree."

"You are welcome, Mr. Caterpillar.
I am glad that I could help."

Busy set out on his way,
feeling less lonely than before.

Next, Busy came upon a big, red ant.
"Hi, Mr. Ant. What are you doing?"

22

"I need to get this piece of grain back to the mound, but it's too big even for me. It will be nighttime before I can drag it back," said the ant.

"Well, I am small but strong," said Busy.
"I will help you get it there."

They worked together as a team to get
the piece of grain back to the mound.

"Oh thank you, Busy.
Now my family
can eat for days,"
said the ant.
"You are a true friend, indeed."

Busy flew on,
feeling not so lonely at all.

26

Busy looked around and saw
all the birds and the bees
and the beetles and all the
creatures in the meadow.

"Wow! Look at this!" said Busy.
"There's a whole little world abuzz,
and I am actually part of it all!

Today, I met new friends, did nice things, and my lonely little meadow turned into a bright, beautiful world!

Doing those kind things made me feel better and helped others, too!"

So...
    When you feel a little lonely,
    or don't know what to do,
    just remember Busy and ...

BE
KIND

Lightning Source UK Ltd.
Milton Keynes UK
UKHW051907070222
398346UK00002B/121